THE BLACK FOREST

Miles Cornelius

I would like to take a moment to dedicate this book to those who have encouraged me over the years. First, my wife of 27 years, Tammy Cornelius. You have always encouraged me, with all of my jobs, going to college, or just taking the time to write, you were always there for me and I dedicate this book to you. To my three children who were the biggest inspirations for the characters in this book. To all of my co-workers at the CAPP Facility as you were the ones who had to read the rough draft. To my friends in high school who suffered through my stories and laughed at every misspelled word therein. You know who you are, and I want to say thank you. To my family and friends who have never given up on me, I want to say thank you.

The intrigue of this book left me thirsty for more!

TY MARLOW

CONTENTS

PROLOGUE

Centuries ago, the black forest was a dark but magical place that was home to many ancient beings who had great power. They used their powers for good to help others who struggled. These beings were enchanted fairies and dwarves, elders of another race. Their humbleness was legendary and their kindness bountiful. But there was a darkness that spread over the land causing the wondrous people of the forest to flee for their lives. An evil came in the shape of a dark and foreboding shadow, a great demon that wanted to rule the land and the people that lived there. His name was Hellmervick. He brought death and destruction to the Black Forest. He wanted to rule the castle of Lavodka that lay to the south of the black forest and keep the enchanted people in captivity.

There were many battles with the demon. He had great power and his hunger for control made him a great adversary. It was only the wisdom of a great and powerful wizard, Kali, who came to the rescue of this land that foiled Hellmervicks' plot. He devised a chamber made of obsidian in which he could capture the demon and imprison him there for eternity.

As long as the trap remained unopened it would hold him. He had to trick the demon into entering the trap of his own free will and this was no easy task, as Hellmervick was very wise. He confronted Hellmervick and told him that the obsidian chamber held the treasure to the black forest, the secret that gave them their magical powers. Hellmervic told him that he would stop at nothing to prevent him from stealing the treasure and destroying their power, rendering them helpless.

Hellmervick believed the wizard and they fought a great battle. Then Hellmervick overpowered Kali, and he was killed. When he entered the chamber, he became trapped and could not escape. The chamber was hidden beneath the roots of a great oak tree by a descendant of Kali, his daughter. Only she knew where the chamber was hidden and did not tell another soul. The story of the great battle was passed down from generation to generation in hopes that no one would ever look for, or uncover the chamber and release Hellmervick back out into the world.

For now, all was safe.

IX

ONE

This is a story about a king, his daughter the princess, a dragon, and a brave knight. Now I know what you are thinking, you have heard stories like this before. A happy kingdom, a princess in distress, and a knight in shining armor comes to her rescue and everyone lives happily ever after. I could even start this story with the usual cliché, like once upon a time, or a long time ago.

But why would I bore you with all that ruckus? As a matter of fact, I won't. I will tell you this, that the adventure that awaits you is something so obscure, so out of the ordinary, that no one would ever dare mention it. They would like to have seen it destroyed, never mentioned, and never spoke of it again. But the facts remain and this story should be told. It should be herald from the highest mountain and put into song so it could be sung about for years to come. Well, maybe not to that extreme. Nonetheless, this story should be passed on from generation to generation so that people will know near and far that we are all alike in every sense of the word. That even though some may struggle, some may have issues, and some may not feel they belong in this world of ours, that they indeed do.

Our story begins upon the princess' twentieth birthday. She was as lovely as the dawning of a new day. Her father the king, a small but brave man, ruled the glorious kingdom of Lavodka. A magnificent castle by the ocean. There many people lived in peace and harmony. But it was not always like this. The kingdom had faced many battles. Other kingdoms wanted to rule over this land, and even a great and powerful demon once tried to destroy the king and rule the land for his own selfish needs. The last fear they faced was a terrible dragon named Dufor that terrorized the kingdom. He was a large, winged dragon that breathed fire and spread hatred among the villagers of the kingdom. The princess' mother, the queen, was once a beautiful woman herself with flowing dark hair. But the dreaded dragon took her and devoured her.

The king had three brave warriors that he sent out to defeat the dragon, but they were unsuccessful. That was many years ago when the princess was only a baby. After the battles with the dragon, it was told that the dragon was bound in a large cave in the mountains of dread that lay just beyond the black forest of the north, an evil place where no one went.

A few months later the king had remarried again. A beautiful woman who had admired the king from the village, had caught his eye. It was not uncommon for a grieving king to find another mate, one that would help fill the void of a passing or lost queen. It was however not a normal practice for the king to find a common woman from his own village. This practice was against the rules of the kingdom. Her name was Esmeralda, a fair-haired young woman who had lived in the village for some time.

The king admired her long golden hair and her figure that he only described as heaven sent. He sent a messenger to the village to invite her to a fabulous feast. He ordered his best hog butchered and dressed for the occasion. There was no way that anyone would refuse the king's invitation, so she accepted. Within a few weeks the two were married. The king felt that he could not raise his daughter on his own, and Esmeralda made a wonderful mother. The king was happy again, and with the dragon bound in the mountains of dread, all seemed well.

The princess was as radiant as ever. She was a lovely woman with long flowing dark hair like her mother, her eyes as green as emeralds, her complexion as white as the driven snow. But living in the kingdom she never had anything to do. There were days when she would talk to the people who lived in the village, but she did not have much in common with them. She was nice to them and would never do anything to harm them as she never thought of herself as better than they were. She was so bored with her daily life, being a princess and all that she called for her favorite jester to liven up her day. "What wilt thou do for me my jester to liven up my day?"

The Jester was a small man, standing only five foot two with radiant red hair. He always wore his favorite costume, a black and white checkered suit made out of the finest linen. Some say that he went as far as the Orient to buy this suit, others said that he weaved it himself out of silk that he gathered. Whatever the case may be, he wore it everywhere he went. He would not perform without it. His performance was almost legionary. He had performed for many kings, his song and dance, and his jokes were unlike any other jester, no matter what kingdom they came from.

But no matter where he went, this was his home. He had come to this kingdom to perform about eight years ago, only being a young lad himself, and when he saw the princess, he made up his mind that this is where he would lay his head. Was he in love with her? Even if he was, that was forbidden, even in this kingdom. She was not in love with any other prince, and she made no issue of it that she even remotely was looking. Some days his heart was bitter because of his feelings, but he continued to do his job and remained friends with the princess only. But today he was feeling a little mischievous and did not feel like entertaining her. He stood before the princess, his head cocked to one side, a fiendish smile on his ashen white face, and in a loud sarcastic voice he said, "No JOKES for you today!" His response angered the princess. She stood to her feet and pointed her finger at the jester. He tilted his head back to an upright position, the faint smile gone from his ashen face.

"You," screamed the princes, her nostrils flaring, "are supposed to be my friend, you are supposed to make me laugh, all you did was insult me you foul creature of the night, you purveyor of rotten jokes, you wart on my father's face, you hider of good lunches, you stealer of everyone's candy, I cast you out of my kingdom to forever reside in the north." The jester opened his mouth to speak again, but nothing came out. His mouth was silent. The princess, her face burning red, spoke up one more time. "What tis the matter jester, has thou something to say?"

The jester, his head hanging low, spoke in a soft tone, "you mean I have to go to the north, where there are evil men that rule the dark forest?" The princes smiled an evil smile and said in a loud voice, "Yes," with an evil laugh, "you will forever reside with those who rule the dark forest of the north." The jester frowned, "but they are plagued with a terrible dragon!" The princes gave no notice to the jester, "What do I care if they walk funny." She called for her guards to take the jester away. She went to stand by the window to look out, still bored out of her mind. The jester, his head still hanging low, walked away with the guards.

There was a knock on the door and the princess looked away from the window. "Enter." She said, dreading that her father would be angry for her action. The door opened and her stepmother walked. "Don't you think you are being a bit harsh on the poor thing my dear?" she said in a dark undertone. The princess thought about it for a moment, then answered her mother.

"Not at all mother dear," a sharp tone in her voice, "I think this would be good for the jester." Esmeralda walked towards her, the smile dying from her face, "You should have had council with your father first, you know the dangers of the black forest and the filthy creatures that inhabit that dark place. Something bad could happen to him you know." The princess looked at her dead in the eyes, "He is supposed to be my friend, for eight years he has entertained me and made me laugh, today all he did was insult me. Why would he do such a thing, why would he insult me this time? I do not understand." She began to sob, her step-mother put a hand on her chin and lifted her face to meet her eyes, "Every man does something silly when they are in love my dear, look at your father and what he did for me. Taking me from the village, bringing me here, making me his queen and your mother, it was like a dream come true, I have never been happier." The princess looked at her squarely, "IN LOVE?" Her eyes now full of fury, "How could such a commoner, a jester, be in love with me? It is not permitted!"

"How could a king be in love with a commoner and marry her, does that same law not apply?" The princess thought about it for a moment, then she turned her head, her face turning a solid red, "I do not love him!" she said, then with that she stormed back to the window. Esmeralda frowned at her, then she turned on her hills and walked briskly out of the room.

TWO

Now legend had it that the dark forest of the north was ruled by three evil men that were once proud citizens of the glorious kingdom. They were Wilber, Fornshell, and Taylor. It was told that once they were the king's bravest warriors and went into many battles with him. They were very rich and had great power over their armies. There were rumors and wild stories of how they wanted to murder the king and take over as rulers of the kingdom. It was because of this hideous plot that they were exiled from the kingdom to forever rule the black forest. There were other stories that they had plotted with the dragon to kill the queen and together they would take over the kingdom for themselves. It was Dylan, the kings' personal sorcerer that told the story of their evil plan and how after learning this knowledge he himself had cast a spell on the warriors and the dragon that they should never hurt the king again.

The princess stood on the balcony, not feeling regret at all for her actions, watched as the guards led the jester out of the castle and across the great lawn. She looked towards the north part of the castle, just beyond a great field she could see the forest and the hills that lay beyond. Just to the left of the forest sat the mountain of dread, a dark and desolate place. It was cold and grey with high jagged peaks.

There was no foliage that grew there and when the sun hit upon it she could see the dark jagged edges and cliffs that seemed to fall into nowhere. She shivered at the sight of it and it seemed that her blood ran cold if only for a moment. She looked again at the jester who appeared as just a small dot on the road, the guards on either side of him. She thought about what her step mother had said, then she thought to herself, did I do the right thing. She shrugged it off and went back inside the castle.

Dylan, the kings' sorcerer, sat in a large chair in a dark cavern just to the left of the castle. His eyes, dark as ever, were looking at, more like piercing, the black crow that had landed inside his domain. He watched it carefully as the crow bobbed around on the floor looking for morsels of food, anything that it could eat. Dylan raised his hand and with a snap the black bird turned to stone. He stood from his chair, standing six foot one he was rather tall, making sure not to hit his head on the low ceiling, he picked up the stone statue that was once a live bird. "Ah, let's see you walk around now you silly crow." He said with a fiendish laugh. He sat the bird on a bookshelf where there were statues of other birds of all types.

"You will look rather good here with your friends." There was a pounding on the door that led to his cavern, a room that he had made out of a stone hillside that lay to the left of the castle before the clearing. He did not like to practice his skill in his chambers of the castle, even though it was a large room, he despised being there. He had moved his lab and potions into his cavern and told everyone that this was where he could think best, without any interruption. "Who could be coming here?" he thought to himself, "I bet it is that stupid jester." He said quietly to himself, mocking the jester in a slight dance as we went to the door.

He opened it ever so slow, making sure not to let in too much light from outside. He smiled at who he saw and bid them welcome and let them inside.

He showed the person to a small chair that sat opposite his own, then with a swift movement he sat down. "We have a problem" said the person who sat across from him. He leaned back in his chair, his hand now on his chin. "And what could this problem be?" He said in a quizzical tone. It was rather dark in his room and only lit by one candle that sat on the table near his book of spells. "It is the jester." The person said, urgency in the voice. "He has been banished to the black forest, and you know what that means"

The sorcerer suddenly stood up. "How could you have let this happen, you fool. Do you know what will happen now, all of my plans, my hard work, it will be destroyed. You should have stopped it." He sounded angry, his face in a grimace. "I may still have time, there is something I can do." He paced back and forth for a moment. "What will you do?" said his visitor. "Oh, I have a plan indeed. You must go now, no one should know you were here." And with that he opened the door.

THREE

"Here we are." Said one of the guards, his voice gruff and agitated. "If I were you I would find shelter as soon as possible, there are strange things here in the black forest." They tossed him aside like he was a bag of potatoes and turned to walk away. "And don't think about trying to come back to the castle mate, I understand that if you do that they will put you in irons and send you off to the dungeon." The other guard said. Then within a matter of minutes they were gone out of view.

The Jester, feeling a bit perplexed, walked into the dark forest. He heard strange noises like the sounds of forks clanging against plates. Suddenly he heard a voice beyond the dark trees. "Hark, who goes there? Friend or Foe?" The Jester, being scared blurted out, "Jester." "Hey, was Jester one of the words?" he heard one voice ask. "No" another voice calmly said. "Its friend or foe, there's no other choice." Said a third voice. One of the voices cleared their throat. "We said friend or foe, there is no other choice."

And with that, the Jester, frightened out of his mind, turned and began to run out of the dark forest when something stepped in his way. The figure was short, about four foot two. He was bald and sported a long gray beard almost like a dwarf. "Did you not hear me, are you friend or foe?" questioned Wilber, a warrior of the dark forest. "I...I....I..."
stuttered the jester as he backed away. Wilber held up a jagged sword, holding it close to the jester he asked his question again.

"F..F...friend!" stuttered the jester, "I was kicked out of the glorious kingdom to be forever banished to the dark woods of the north." "Have you come to help us?" asked Fornshell who suddenly appeared next to Wilber. The jester looked at them again, how could they be so menacing when they were so short? "We have had a problem with a terrible dragon!" exclaimed Taylor, who also appeared to the left of Fornshell.

"I heard," said the Jester, "don't they have corrective shoes for that?" They looked at each other puzzled when suddenly Fornshell pointed his finger and shouted, "Thar she blows, oh wait, this isn't a pirate story." He cleared his throat, "look, it's the dreaded dragon Dufor donning deadly dungeon dice!!" Everyone looked at Fornshell, he smiled faintly, "I don't know," he said shrugging his shoulders, "it just sounded cool." The dragon, a large winged creature, swooped towards the four hapless people as they ran into the woods. The dragon turned towards the woods and with a ferocious roar breathed fire at them as they disappeared into their layer. The dragon tried to go into the woods, but he was halted by a force that would not let him enter. He tried again, and again he bounced off of what seemed to be an invisible wall. This made Dufor angry and he took off, heading for the village.

They took the jester to their layer deep with-in the forest. As they walked along the jester asked, "Why are you here? There are a lot of wild stories about you?" Fornshell answered, "There are some things that cannot be explained in a short story and this is one of them." "Surely there must be some truth to the story?" the jester asked. "No, well maybe just a little, but not a whole lot, well maybe more than we want to admit to." Added Taylor in an unsure voice.

"Most folk call this place the dark forest of the north, but we prefer to call it the black forest, deep inside there are magical mystical wondrous things." Said Wilber in a dry voice, "You see," he continued, "when we first came here we were outcasts. There were other outcasts here as well and they showed us many of the things we may show you. I only say may because we do not know yet as to why you are here, and with the dragon awakening recently we have been worried that he is sending others here to harm us. You see, he cannot enter into the black forest, not only is it forbidden, but there is a magical barrier that was created long ago. You know the dragon is as old as time itself. And of course, you know the legend of the powerful demon Hellmervick.

The enchanted creatures that were here have passed on and left the knowledge of the black forest to us so that if the dragon gains more power we will be able to defeat him." The jester shook his head, "But if the dragon has been bound these many years, how did he get loose?" "We do not know, we just know that he is loose and he has an agenda." Fornshell said with a bit of bewilderment in his voice.

They all stopped walking, the jester looked ahead in amazement. Before them was a large door fastened to the side of the hill. It was covered in ivy with strange blooms and golden flowers as such the jester had never seen before. Taylor opened the large door with a mighty push and the jester peeked inside. There before him was a large room hollowed out of the side of the hill. There was a large oak table with chairs around it. On the table were various candles that illuminated the room. He looked to his left and there saw other furnishing to sit on with more candles and lanterns. To his right was a large wooden desk, more candles that were lit sat upon it. On the walls he saw drawings, one in particular caught his eye.

It was of the castle, a dark figure hovered over the castle. Just to the left looked like a drawing of the princess full grown bound to a pillar, fire under her feet. Then he saw it, a small figure drawn next to the right of the castle. It was a man with bright red hair, a sword in one hand and a bright red glowing object around his neck. He stood there frozen, chills going up and down his back as if someone had just walked on his grave. Wilber saw him shake, "Are you alright?" he asked. The jester looked at him, his ashen white face now pale as if he had seen a ghost, "I am not sure," he said, "that painting, how long has that been on the wall?" Wilber looked at the wall then back at the jester, "We were told that it was painted long ago, the foreshadowing of something terrible." The jester took a step back, his face pale, his eyes almost sunken into his skull, "This can't be happening to me!"

FOUR

The village that lay just south of the castle of the glorious kingdom was filled with happy people. The village lay near the ocean where it was always sunny and warm. Today was like any other day, the villagers were doing their chores, the children were playing, and all seemed well. That was until a great shadow appeared over the village, a shadow in the shape of a great dragon. Dufor appeared and began breathing fire, burning their homes. "The dreaded dragon Dufor has returned!" yelled one of the villagers, "run for your lives!" The villagers ran for cover, hiding where they could to get away from the awful dragon. "What has made you come back after all this time?" shouted another villager. The dragon stopped and looked at him, hate burning in his eyes, "It is the princess' twentieth birthday," said the dragon in his whiny voice, "It's time to show everyone who is boss around here, and you shall wish you was never born!" snorted the dragon. With that he breathed fire upon the rest of the village, burning it to the ground.

The princess sat in her large room, still really bored, thinking about how she treated the jester. All of a sudden there was a loud commotion outside. She walked over to the window to look out, all of the people of the kingdom were clamoring at the gates of the castle. She opened the window to listen and heard them shouting in a low toneless voice.... "Clamor, clamor, clamor clamor clamor." Just as she shut the window her father the king walked in. "Father, what is wrong with the villagers, they are revolting." "I know, I saw them," shivered the King, "but the dragon has destroyed their village, what shall we do?" "I know" exclaimed the princess, "We will hire a great knight to help us rid our kingdom of the dragon "Ah," said the king, "But where shall we find such a brave soul?" She was about to tell her father, the king, where they could find a brave soul when suddenly and without warning the writer of the story got writer's block. Both the king and princess stood there with their mouths open, staring at each other not knowing what to say.

Finally, the princes spoke, "I have an idea, we could call for the rulers of the dark forest of the north. I hear that they have tools and skills that can help us defeat the dragon." Just at that moment they heard a great roar as the dragon appeared at the window and in a weird whiny voice said, "go ahead and try to find them, try to get them here, try to get them to defeat me, try and get them to come here already, they won't!" and with that he grabbed the princess and flew away. The king clutched his chest in agony.

The door to the princess room burst open and Esmeralda stood in the doorway. "What happened?" she asked in a shocked voice. The king stood there, tears streaming down his face. "The dragon." He stammered, she could hear the fear in his voice. "He has taken my daughter." "The dragon?" her voice quivering, she ran towards the king and flung her arms around him. With confusion in her voice she spoke again. "But he has been bound these many years, how could he have escaped Dylan's spell?" The king shook his head, trying to fight back more tears, "I do not know. Did you not know he torched the village? He has come back to wreak his revenge on us, he has taken my daughter, I have got to save her." Esmeralda put his face to her chest, she stroked his hair lovingly, her eyes seemed to look off in the distance. "Don't worry my husband, there is no need to worry." She looked down at him and smiled.

The king, being grief stricken with the kidnapping of his daughter, called his council to order. They met in the large dining hall in the south side of the castle. The council was made up of his four bravest knights, his bishop, and his sorcerer Dylan who wore his bright red robe. His hair was long and grey, and he sported a thin mustache that almost livened up his face. "What are we to do? The dragon is back and has kidnapped my daughter. I do not want to see the dragon devour her as he did my wife so long ago."

They all looked towards the sorcerer, he stared back at them, his eyes gleaming, his nostrils flaring. "Well don't look at me. Why is it every time a dragon appears all the king's men want the sorcerer to do something?" "Oh I know," he continued in a sarcastic voice, "the sorcerer has powers, he could change him into a frog or something like that! Well let me tell you something, I am not that kind of sorcerer, I am no Merlin and I am certainly not a magician, so don't look at me to solve your little problem. Last time it was a mere fluke that anything happened at all, I just work here!" And with that he turned and stormed out of the room.

'Well now that we got rid of him, what shall we do?" said the king. They all thought for a moment. Then the king remembered something his daughter had said just before she was taken. "By Jove I've got it! We will call for the warriors of the black forest!" shouted the king. His subjects jumped in surprise. His bishop, a rather large man with a flowing white beard spoke up, "But wouldn't it be dangerous to call on them? I mean after all, didn't they want to kill you once?" "Well," started the king, "that's not really what happened, but I don't have time to go into details right now. Nicholas," the king said, "you are by far the bravest knight in the whole Kingdom, I will ask you to take on the task of finding the warriors and giving them this proclamation." "What if they refuse?" Nicholas asked in a strange Scottish voice. The king looked at him, a frown settling on his face. "Then we shall have to take war with the dragon ourselves and get back my daughter before that fiendish dragon has lunch with her, and I don't mean in a nice way."

FIVE

The jester sat in a large chair looking over what was to be his new home. He frowned. In the castle he had his own chambers, granted it was not as nice as the princess chambers, which he had only seen once and purely by accident.

He had been coming back from a long journey entertaining in other villages and was extremely tired. At least this is what his story was. He entered the castle and took a wrong turn, then next thing he knew he was in the princess' chamber. He remembered how fine the linen was, how sweet the room smelled. He let his mind wander back to the princess face, her delicate features. Then he stopped, he had to remind himself that he was only a jester, what could he offer the princess? "Nothing." He thought to himself. Yet he could not deny the feeling that he was in love with her. How could he have done this to her when all he was trying to do was be funny for her. "I should have done things differently, then I wouldn't be in this horrible God forsaken place with would be murderers." He said to himself.

He looked up and noticed that Taylor was sitting across from him angrily staring at him. "So you are a jester huh?" Taylor asked. "How long you been doing that gig?" The jester thought for a moment then spoke, "Since I was just a young lad of about 14, my father was a jester, and his father was a jester." "And what of your father before that?" Taylor asked. "Oh he was a knight, he didn't know how to be funny." "Enough of this small talk," said Fornshell in a seemingly irritated voice, "what we really want to know is why you are here, who sent you and what is your real purpose?"

All three of them were now looming over the jester. He gulped in a breath of air, then went into his story of how he had hurt the feelings of the princess. The three of them looked at him in astonishment, looked at each other, then they all laughed out loud.

"So, she sent you here? How foolish was that?" shouted Wilber, his face in a twisted laugh that almost made it look like his eyeballs would pop out at any second. The jester had to look away as he felt his stomach turn. "And what did they tell you, that you needed to find shelter, that the strange inhabitants would eat you alive?" said Taylor. "It's all poppycock of course, we are not nearly as bad as all that." Then Taylor stood to his feet. "Listen lad, if there is one thing you should know, it is this. We have lived here in the forest for twenty years. That darn dragon is what put us here." "And we almost had him too!" added Fornshell. "But if you want to know the truth, it was that stupid sorcerer of the king that did it. He blundered with his stupid spell. He not only tarnished our reputation, but when he bound the dragon to the caves in the mountain of dread, he bound us here as well!"

"Of course, he is the one that started all the wild rumors about us. We wouldn't hurt one strand of hair on that poor king's head of his." Said Wilber, his voice agitated at the thought. "So that is why you have not left the forest?" exclaimed the jester, "that is why you have not come back? This makes so much more sense, that sorcerer is just horrible." "Not only that," exclaimed Fornshell, "but he put a curse on the princess, if by her 20th birthday if she has not fallen in love with him, the dragon would be free. We have to work fast to come up with a plan." The jester stood to his feet, "what shall we do?" he asked in excitement. "We have a few things up our sleeves." At that moment there was a small alarm that had went off. "Someone is approaching the forest." Wilber said looking in alarm. "Let's not make haste, we will go and see who it is, jester, you stay here" "Oh no" said the jester, "I am going with you!" The three of them looked at the jester, looked at each other, then in they all left together.

When Nicholas reached the black forest, he entered cautiously. He heard a strange sound like forks clanging on plates. Suddenly he heard a voice from the darkness.

"Hark, who goes there, friend or foe?" "Friend," Nicholas said nervously with a strange Scottish accent, "I am looking for the rulers of the dark forest, I have a proclamation from the king." "Go on." The voice from the darkness said. Nicholas spoke again, "I, the king of the glorious kingdom, hereby bequeath you to come to the kingdom and defeat Dufor the dreaded dragon, if you accept this mission, you will be granted riches beyond belief." The three rulers and the jester walked out into the clearing. The jester looked at Nicholas and spoke, "I will defeat Dufor the dreaded dragon dealing dismay to downtrodden townsfolk of the glorious kingdom!" Wilber, Fornshell, and Taylor looked at the jester in astonishment. "You will?" all three of them cried. "Yes" said the jester, a smile on his face, "I will go into battle." "But you were abolished from the glorious kingdom," said Wilber, "why would you risk life and limb for them?"

The jester thought for a moment, when there arose such a mighty wind, and to their surprise the dragon appeared. "So you think you can slay me? You are nothing more than a jester, and not a good one at that!" snorted the dragon in his weird whiny voice, "I will not only roast you, but your friends as well!" With that he gave a strange laugh and flew away. Nicholas looked at the jester, "I knight thee jester and hereby deputize thee to the fullest extent of the law and hereby bequeath you the deed of defeating the dreaded dragon Dufor."

The jester turned to the rulers of the dark forest, "You must train me, you have skills and tools that I do not possess." Wilber, Fornshell, and Taylor agreed. They took the jester back to their secret layer deep within the dark forest. Wilber spoke first, "Remember I told you we had a few things that were given to us. This is a special sword, when used correctly it will help you defeat the dragon." And he handed the jester a golden sword. Fornshell spoke next, "This is a special amulet, when worn around the neck it will protect thee from harm." Taylor spoke next, "I give you words of wisdom, do not listen to the dragon, he will try and deceive you with his lies."

The Jester looked at Taylor in surprise, "Don't you have any kind of weapon for me?" The Jester asked. "Alas," said Taylor, "I do not, as I am only a weekend warrior, and since this is Thursday, I got nothing." Wilber spoke again, "Listen lad, we were all once great warriors and led our own forces for the king. But that is another story that will be shared another time." Wilbur looked towards the heavens, then spoke again in a harsh tone, "When using the sword you must say, by the power of the dark forest and it will glow. You can use it then to wound the dragon." Fornshell spoke up, "That amulet you have will also glow a ruby red color and protect thee from harm." Taylor spoke, "if none of that works, run!" Then the jester bid farewell to the rulers and headed towards the glorious kingdom.

SIX

Esmeralda sat on her throne, a large, beautiful chair fashioned just for the queen. She was thinking about how she was going to rule the kingdom if anything ever happened to her husband the king. This thought brought a large smile across her face. This caused lines to break on her smooth and silky skin. She even laughed to herself a bit, then the smile went away as she thought how impractical this was, even if the dragon was loose and taking his revenge. Would he devour the princess as he did her mother? This thought brought a wrinkle to her almost perfect nose.

Would he destroy the castle now that the village was in ruin? She was interrupted in thought as Dylan approached her throne. "What can I do for thee sorcerer?" She asked in an almost sinister voice. "The dragon, I know he has laid waste to the village and kidnapped the princess. What shall you have me do my queen?" She pondered this question for a moment. When she spoke it was with such authority you would have thought she came from a long line of royalty. "You will do nothing as you stated in your meeting with the council. We have sent a brave knight into the black forest to summon the rulers there. They shall take care of this mess that you obviously bungled twenty years ago. Now leave me at peace while I think of what to do with you." The sorcerer looked at her, his eyes meeting hers. With an elegance that he had not shown before, he smiled and bowed at her, then went on his way.

When the jester reached the glorious kingdom, he had found the dragon had torched the place. He discovered that the dragon had also kidnapped the princess and took her to his hideout, a cave near the mountains of dread. When he reached the mouth of the cave he stood there and spoke in a loud voice, "Dufor, the dreaded dragon, I have come to defeat you and rescue the princess, I am hereby deputized." The dragon stepped out of the cave, in his whiny voice said, "What? You think you can defeat me, a dragon?" With that, the jester raised the sword and said in a loud voice, "By the power of the dark forest!" and the sword began to glow. With this the dragon reared back and took in a deep breath, smoke and fire billowed from his open mouth, but the amulet glowed red and deflected the fire. The jester lunged at the dragon with the glowing sword high in the air, the dragon lunged at the jester. As they collided, he thrust the sword into the dragon's arm and Dufor let out a whiny cry. The jester drew out shackles and put them on the dragon.

He rushed into the cave, there tied to a post was the princess. She smiled when she saw the jester, her heart full of love and regret for her actions. He loosened her straps and wrapped his arms around the princess. "I am so sorry for kicking you out of the kingdom, I had no real cause to do that." Said the princess in a low soft voice. The jester looked at her, his eyes full of love, "awe, that's okay, it helped me to be brave." They embraced in a long passionate kiss and they walked out of the mouth of the cave together, hand in hand.

When he reached the kingdom with the princess he was met at the gate by the sorcerer. "Awe, how sweet, you have brought the princess back, there must be a handsome reward for her, surely?" Dylan said in a weird whiny voice, walking closer to the princess and the jester.
The jester thought his voice sounded different, but he had talked to the sorcerer many times and his voice never sounded like this. "Not so fast," warned the jester, "I know all about you." The princess looked at the jester in surprise. Dylan stood before the jester, his face in a grimace. "And what do you know?" he asked, his voice now low and dark, like the sound of a sword being sharpened.

"I have been with Wilber, Fornshell, and......" the sorcerer cut him off, "lies, I tell you, they lie like rugs." "What are you talking about jester? Dylan is my friend." Asked the princess, confusion in her voice. "Oh, didn't you know? He is in love with you, and he put a curse on you if you did not reciprocate." The princess pushed herself away from the jester, a frown on her face. "That is a lie, I should have never let you get near me." She walked over to Dylan who put his hand on her shoulder. "You can never trust these jesters, foolish people really."

There was a sound of thunder overhead and the jester looked up. Dark clouds had begun to form around the castle. "I want to thank you my boy for bringing the princess back." Said the sorcerer as he began to back away with the princess. "Her father will be happy to see her alive and well, and oh for your reward....." He lifted his right hand and thrust it towards the jester, a bolt of blue lightning emitted from his fingertips, and it hit the jester. He flew back onto the ground with a loud thud, rolling in agony. He looked as if he was dead. "Oh don't worry about him, he is merely unconscious." The princess looked sharply at the sorcerer, "what can I say" he said shrugging his shoulders, "you have always been mine since birth." And with that he grabbed his robe and thrust it around the princess and in a puff of smoke they were both gone.

SEVEN

The jester awoke to find that he had been taken back to the black forest. He jumped up only to have Taylor put his hand on his shoulder. "Easy lad," Taylor said calmly. "How did I get back here if you guys can't leave?" Taylor removed his hand, Wilber and Fornshell walked over to him. "We didn't, we found you outside." The jester looked furious, "Dylan!" he shouted. The three of them looked at each other in surprise then looked at the jester. "The sorcerer, what about him?" asked Taylor. "He took the princess, he hit me with a bolt of lightning, that's the last I remember."

With that, the jester stood to his feet. "Whoa now, we can't just go running out into that storm." "Storm?" the jester thought to himself, then he remembered the dark clouds. "But I need to save the princess, I need your help!" The three of them looked at each other again. Wilber stood up and walked over to a small chest that sat on the floor next to the table. He took a key from around his neck and gingerly unlocked the chest. When he opened it, a bright light emitted from inside of it. The jester looked in astonishment as Wilber took out a small glowing scepter.

"What is that?" The jester asked. Wilber walked back over towards the jester. "This my young friend is our answer. Remember, I told you that the inhabitants that were here before had magical mystical powers. This golden scepter can take off the curse and allow us to leave here." Fornshell spoke next, "it gives us the power to go beyond the barrier that was put here by Dylan years ago that held us inside, and we just loved it here so much we never wanted to leave." The jester watched as all three of them touched the glowing scepter. Once all three of them held onto it the bright orange glow changed to a bright purple glow covering all three of them. Then without warning, there was a flash of bright light that illuminated the entire chambers and as suddenly as it came, the light was gone. Wilber, Fornshell, and Taylor stood before the jester, the once small men were now at least six feet tall.

They were adorned in battle gear, their muscles large, and swords were hanging from their sides. The jester blinked at this sight; he could not comprehend what had just happened.

The three of them looked at each other, they looked down at themselves, feeling their bodies, then they looked at each other again, smiles on their gruff faces. "Ah, it is good to be back to normal." Wilber said as he grabbed onto his sword. The other two agreed and then they walked over to the jester who was still in amazement. "We have no time to lose," said Fornshell as he walked towards the door. "Wait!" shouted Wilber, "we have no clue where he would have taken the princess." Fornshell stopped dead in his tracks then turned towards the jester. "Don't look at me," the jester said, "I have no idea where he took her. For all I know he could have taken her to his dark cavern where he likes to go when he is "thinking" about things." Fornshell, Wilber, and Taylor looked at the jester, their jaws slack, their eyes moving back and forth in their skull. "And just where would this dark cavern be?" asked Wilber, with a hint of sarcasm. The jester sat back down then looked up at the three warriors, "that's just it, I have only been there once, and I really don't know." The three warriors sat in their chairs, looks of defeat on their face when suddenly the jester leaned forward, his eyes wide.

Wait, I've got it!" The three looked at him in surprise, eagerness in their eyes as they waited for him to finish. "Just outside the castle to the left, there is a small hillside, I remember going there with the sorcerer once, a long time ago. He said that it was his special place where he liked to go and think. He had made a cavern out of it in the stone, there is a large door there as well. I think he has a laboratory in there where he makes his potions for his spells." The three warriors stood to their feet. "Well then, what are we waiting for?" said Taylor with the other two speaking almost in harmony. They opened the door and to their surprise the storm was so fierce that it flung the door shut in their faces. "The storm is bad, maybe we should wait." Fornshell said as a look of disappointment came onto his face.

The jester walked past them and opened the door again with a mighty shove. "There is no time to wait, we must act now!" and with that, the jester walked into the storm, Fornshell, Wilber, and Taylor following.

As they left the black forest they came across the mountain of dread. The jester looked and saw the shackles he had placed on the dragon laying on the ground, a look of horror came across his face. "What's wrong?" shouted Wilber over the wind. "The dragon, I left him here bound, but he is gone." "Didn't you slay him?" Asked Wilber. "No, I was going to have the knights come and get him. Something's not right." Said the jester, a look of confusion on his face. Bending over to look at the shackles he suddenly straightened up. He looked at the warriors, "You said that you had been here for 20 years, bound right?" They shook their heads. "And you said you had not seen or heard of the dragon, that he had been bound for 20 years, yes?' Again, they shook their head.

"Tell me, when you went to defeat the dragon after he devoured the Queen, was it just the three of you?" They looked at each other, then Wilber spoke, "No, the sorcerer came with us too, but when we reached the black forest we got separated. We fought with the dragon, but we could not defeat him." A look of hatred came on his face. "The dragon disappeared, and Dylan showed up, he started doing his mumbo jumbo and the next thing we knew we were trapped in the black forest, all our strength gone, short and unable to leave. He apologized and tried to reverse it, but it didn't work. Then he said that it was meant for the dragon, but it must have trapped all of us." The jester looked towards the mouth of the cave. "And he has been there the whole time, just like you in the black forest?" They all shook their heads. "Except for one thing, when I went in there to rescue the princess, there was nothing, no sign of a dwelling area, no food, no water, nothing. If he had been in there for twenty years, there was no sign of it."

The jester stopped, the look on his face changed from bewilderment and the expression became one of understanding. He looked at the three warriors who were still very confused. His eyes widened, "We gotta go!" he shouted, and they all headed towards the castle.

EIGHT

When they reached the castle, it was blazing. The smoke and ash from the smoldering blaze filled their nostrils with a foul stench. Smoked billowed as they stood there taking in the damage. Part of the north wall was gone and most of the castle that was not on fire was in rubble. Except for the king's chambers and the south part of the castle, which still stood without damage. On the ground ahead of them lay a figure, as they approached, they saw it was the king. Rushing to his side, the jester knelt and took the kings hand. "Tell me, what happened?" asked the jester. The king looked up at him, fright in his eyes. "Dufor, the dragon."

He could barely speak, his face burned, his clothes torn to shreds. "He took his revenge on us, I believe he has killed Esmeralda as well, where is my daughter?" The jester looked at him with pity in his eyes. He could hardly stand to tell him the truth. "She is in good hands, do not worry about the dragon, I know how to slay him." The king gave the jester a faint smile, then closed his eyes forever. The jester folded the king's hands over his chest then stood up and drew the sword that the three warriors had given him. He looked at them as they stood there mourning the death of the king. "We shall be sad for him another day, but as of now we have bigger fish to fry." He began walking towards the north end of the castle, Wilber, Fornshell, and Taylor swiftly on his heels.

The storm had become more violent, and rain began to pour on the jester and the three warriors. The smell of the fire in the castle mixed with the rain hitting the dry Earth floated into their nostrils as they rounded the North side of the castle. The jester stopped dead in his tracks. He thought he saw a figure standing in front of them, but the rain was so heavy now and coming at him sideways he could not tell. He lifted his hands to his eyes and rubbed them to see if he could see better. There was someone standing before him, it was a knight adorned in shiny armour, a large steel blade in his right hand. "I have come to help do battle with you and your warriors." It was Nicholas, he had been on the Queens business when the dragon wreaked havoc on the castle and village. "The dragon has taken the princess, again, this time he is not far, he did not go back to the mountains of dread. Follow me, he is this way." With that, Nicholas turned and began to walk towards the back side of the castle. There lay the green hills of Talack, beyond that was the vast emptiness that lay between this kingdom and the valley beyond.

It was hard to see; the darkness of the clouds and the rain had made vision beyond a few feet barely visible. Every so often there would be a flash of lightning that would illuminate the hillside and the river to the east. As they made their way past the first few hills, the jester noticed what appeared to be a small fire in the distance. He wondered how a fire could still be blazing with all this rain. Suddenly Nicholas stopped, he began starring in the distance. The jester, Wilber, Fornshell, and Taylor all stopped as well, peering into the darkness beyond to try and see what Nicholas was looking at. There was a sudden flash of lightning and for a brief moment they saw the princess tied to a stake, a small fire in a pit to the left of her. There was another flash of lightning and suddenly Dylan appeared as if from nowhere. When he did the thunder cracked with a deafening boom that made the ground shudder. Lightning struck a nearby tree, flames and sparks emitting from the branches as the tree split in two. The sorcerer gleamed at the jester, his eyes like balls of fire. It seemed as if he could look right through him and it made the jester shudder.

The sorcerer moved his eyes to focus on the three warriors, a sneer came across his face. His made his whole countenance look evil.

He raised his finger to the three warriors and spoke, his voice now as loud and booming as the thunder they had just heard. "What are you doing here," he roared, anger in his voice, "I thought I settled your hash last time?" Wilber took a step forward, "Did you think we would stay in that blasted forest forever? We have been waiting for this moment for twenty years!" And with that he raised his sword.

The sorcerer sneered and with an evil laugh he raised his right hand, bolts of lightning illuminated from his fingertips hitting Wilber with a massive strike. Wilber flew back, his body thudding against the ground. With that, Taylor lunged towards the sorcerer, but was met with the same fierce bolt of lightning. The others stood there as the sorcerer laughed, the evil grin on his face widening. "There is nothing you can do to harm me, as you can see I am much more powerful than you would ever hope to imagine."

The jester looked down feeling hopeless, a sense of defeat coming over his body. He looked at Fornshell who quickly stepped to the jester's side. "Fear not jester, for I still have the golden scepter, if used right it will give us great power to use against him." Fornshell patted the scepter that was attached to his side. "There is something about him that scares me, I believe he and the dragon to be working together," the jester said as his eyes scanned the heavens, "I have felt this since we found the dragon loose from his Shackles." Nicholas backed up towards the jester and Fornshell so he could hear the conversation. He looked sharply at the jester. "What is this you say, you believe them to be working together?"

The jester shook his head. "I know I have only been in the kingdom a short while, but I made friends with Dylan when I first arrived here. He did not seem this evil. As a matter of fact he appeared to be a kind of fool." The other two shook their heads in agreement. Dylan watched them closely as the three of them huddled together. "Going over some secret plan?" he hissed in a whiny voice. The jester jerked back, that voice he thought to himself, where had he heard that voice before.

Wilber and Taylor began to stumble to their feet, the shock starting to wear off of them. Nicholas walked over and helped the two of them as they steadied themselves. "What is our plan?" whispered Taylor. "We have no plan." Nicholas said as he helped them walk to where the jester and Fornshell stood. The rain began to let up and they could see a little more clearly now. They noticed that the princess, while tied to a stake, was completely unconscious, kindling lay just below her feet as if she were to be burned alive. The four of them huddled together and began to talk.

"Fornshell, so you have the golden scepter?" asked Wilber with concern in his voice. Fornshell patted his side where the scepter rested. Wilber shook his head. "What can you do with this?" asked Nicholas. "We can use it to make us stronger and attack Dylan, Jester, do you still have the sword we gave you and the amulet?" The jester took out the sword, but when he felt around his neck the amulet was gone. "Looking for this?" hissed Dylan as he held the ruby red amulet up by his left hand. The jester looked at the amulet, then back at Dylan. "You swine, you thief of innocent youth, you ugly puss filled wart on the backside of a mule, how dare you steal my amulet!"

The jester shouted; hate filled in his voice. With that the sorcerer took the amulet and thrust it into his palm. He brought his two hands together with a loud crash and the amulet shattered into a thousand pieces. The sorcerer let out a ferocious roar. Thunder boomed and lightning struck the sky again. With that all four of them turned towards the sorcerer, the golden scepter now glowing a bright red color. All four of them touched it and they were immediately covered in a bright amber glow. The glow illuminated the whole hillside and there was a sudden flash of orange light. The sorcerer watched in amazement as the four of them drew their swords.

The four of them charged at the sorcerer, Wilber to his left, Fornshell to his right. The jester and Nicholas head on. The sorcerer waved his hand as they descended on him causing a cloud of black smoke. He suddenly vanished as the four of them came to a head. They stopped dead in their tracks and began to look around. "I should have seen that one coming" yelled Taylor as he turned to see the sorcerer was now behind them. "How are we going to fight him without magic?" asked the jester, now feeling that maybe this was a bad idea. "I have a few things up my sleeve." Wilber stated as he grabbed the golden scepter. "By the power of the black forest!" he exclaimed as he held it above his head. A bolt of lightning hit the scepter and it began to glow a dark green color. Suddenly spirits arose from the ground and began to go inside the scepter, and it grew into a large pointed arrow. With all his might he thrust the scepter at the sorcerer. The sorcerer tried to leap back but the scepter pierced him in the chest. Dylan flew backwards and hit the ground with a thud. He groaned as he lay there. The four of them cheered as they saw the sorcerer take his last breath.

NINE

Nicholas patted Wilber on the back, "You did it old friend." He said with a smile. Wilber looked at the jester, "if it wasn't for the jester, he helped us get our strength back." He smiled at the jester who in turn smiled back. The jester then looked at the princess who was starting to moan a little and wake up. He approached her and smiled. "Hmm," he smiled, "somehow this looks familiar." The princess looked down at him and she smiled. The jester moved around to the back of her and began to loosen her binds. As he did he heard a great rumbling sound.

Nicholas, Taylor, Fornshell, and Wilber, who were in front of the princess to help her down from the stake, also heard the sound. They looked at each other then looked up at the princess, her face turning from a smile to a state of shock. They turned to look in the direction she was looking and to their horror they saw what she saw. The sorcerer stood to his feet, a scowl widened across his face. He grabbed the scepter that was stuck in his chest and ripped it out, making no sound as he did so. But as they looked it seemed that his chest was expanding. They watched and gasped as the sorcerer bent over, seemingly in pain, but as they watched wings burst out of his back. He stood to an upright position again and his face was twisted in an agonizing smile.

His chest thrust again, and his feet began to change into what looked like large toes with claws on the end of them. He coughed and blood spewed from his mouth as it began to take on another shape. Horns burst from his forehead. The jester, frozen in fear, re-positioned his composer and finished untying the princess. As she came off the stake Nicholas took her hand and helped her down.

"Run." Said Taylor to the princess. "Go and seek shelter now, while you still have time." He looked towards the rolling hills. She shook her head. Before she left she turned to the jester, "how could I have doubted you." She said lovingly, she took the jesters hand and leaned into his face to give a small kiss. The jester gently kissed her back, then gently pushed her away and looked towards the hills. She smiled and with that she began to run.

The jester turned to Wilber, "Now what?" Wilber shrugged and they turned their attention towards the sorcerer. The four of them stood in amazement, Dufor the dragon now stood before them. He snarled and breathed in with all his might. The four of them knew what this meant, and they scrambled in different directions as the dragon breathed out smoke and flames. When the fire was gone Dufor looked but could not see the four of them. He flapped his large mighty wings and flew into the air. As the dragon circled around looking for them, they huddled together behind a large rock formation that was attached to one of the hillsides.

The jester turned to Wilber, "I guess I was wrong, Dylan and Dufor aren't working together, it looks like they are one. How will we defeat him?" Wilber looked at the jester, then he looked at his fellow comrades. Fornshell, Taylor, and Nicholas looked exhausted, a blank expression on their faces. He turned back towards the jester. "You are our only hope. You still have the golden sword, you are the only one that can defeat him." The jester looked down at the sword in his hand, then looked back at Wilber. "Go find the princess, get her back to the black forest, take them with you," he pointed to the other three, "I will stay here and fight the dragon." Wilber shook his head. With that, the jester ran out and into the open. He saw Dufor searching the hillsides for them.

He clutched the sword and raised it above his head about to say the charm that gave the sword its power. Before he could speak the words, the sword began to glow and vibrate in his hand. At this Dufor saw him and headed towards him. He flew down on him and with his enormous claw he grabbed the jester. "I have you now" Dufor roared. Wilber saw this and shuddered. He had found the princess and they were starting to head back towards the black forest, but when they saw this they stopped.

The dragon spoke again, "I do not know how you did not know that we were one in the same. But now you will feel what it is like to be a side of beef roasting before a great feast!" The dragon let out a howl as if he were trying to laugh. The jester, firmly tight in the clutch of the dragon's claw looked down and saw the warriors and the princess. They had stopped so they could watch what was happening. He tried to reposition himself so he could see the dragons' chest, the glowing sword still vibrating in his right hand. Every time he would move, the dragon would tighten his grip. Dufor also saw that the four of them had stopped to watch, and he thought to himself that he could take this opportunity to kill them as well. As he swooped towards them he took in a deep breath of air. The jester looked frantically, he had to do something, or his friends and the princess would be roasted.

With his left hand free, he stealthily took a grip on the dragon's talon. Forcing himself into an upright position without giving the dragon an idea that he was shifting, he now faced the dragons' chest. He gripped the sword with both hands and with all of the strength he could muster, he shoved the sword deep into Dufors chest. As the sword ripped apart the flesh, the jester could see that the sword had penetrated the dragon's heart. Dufor let out a great cry and his wings quit flapping. He struggled to stay in the air as the jester forced the sword deeper into his chest. The dragon lost his balance, still clutching tightly to the jester, he twirled in midair. He let out another cry, "You stupid fool." The warriors and the princess watched in horror as the dragon began to descend very fast to the ground. Almost spinning out of control, the jester began to get very dizzy as he tried to free himself from Dufors deadly grip. Dufor let out another cry as the sword ripped through his heart. The jester could see what looked like a beam of light as the sword opened his heart. As they sped towards the ground the warriors and the princess gasped as they too saw the bright beam, and in an instant the dragon exploded seconds before they hit the ground.

"Oh no!" cried the princess as she began to rush to where the fragments of what was once the dragon began to fall onto the earth. The foul stench in the air of burning flesh hung heavy as the princess approached the body that lay before her. Nicholas, Wilber, Fornshell, and Taylor, shock still on their faces, began to run after her. Dodging bits of dragon flesh, the princess began to cry fearing that the jester too had perished in the strange explosion. The main part of Dufors body lay on the ground still intact. As she approached the giant claw she could see the jester. He was still in the clutch of the claw and he lay motionless. She put her hands up to her face, tears now streaming down the sides of her delicate cheeks. Nicholas put his hand on her shoulder, choking back the tears, he tried to comfort her. "He was, is, the bravest man I have ever met." The other warriors agreed as they looked down at the jester. The sword was gone, his hands empty.

"That blast must have killed him." Said Wilber as he looked at his two friends. The princess gave one last look as she wiped the tears from her eyes, then she and the four warriors turned to walk away. As they began to walk back to the castle, they heard a strange, muffled noise that almost sounded like a cough

TEN

The princess turned her head and looked in the direction where the dragon lay on the ground, still smoldering. She saw a rustling and her eyes lit up. She turned around, now completing facing the dragon and then she saw it, the jester was moving. Swiftly, she ran back towards the jester, her heart felt like it was jumping into her throat. As she approached, she saw the jester, coughing and wheezing as he tried to free himself from the claw of the dragon. He noticed the princess and turned to look at her, "I see you are alright." The jester said with a cough.

She smiled at him; her smile as bright as the morning sun. The jester was still struggling when he saw the warriors advance upon the dragon's' claw and helped to pry it open. As the jester tried to stand, he stumbled a little and fell into Wilber's arms. Wilber steadied him, "You alright?" Wilber asked. The jester looked at him, his red hair singed by the mighty burst. "I believe so, at least I am for now." Wilber steadied him back on his feet, then placed his large right hand on the jester's shoulder, "I would follow you into battle anywhere brave knight." The jester looked at Wilber in amazement. "You are the knight, not I, I am just a jester." Nicholas spoke up, "Umm, no, if you remember right, I was given the power to knight you from the king himself." Suddenly they all realized what had happened to the king and they all bowed their heads in remembrance of him.

The princess looked at the jester gingerly, her eyes fell upon his face and as she put her arms around him she spoke in a soft voice, "I should have never doubted you, after all, you are my most favorite jester in the whole world." With this she gave him a kiss.

Wilber, Fornshell, and Taylor looked at each other then looked at the jester. "What?" said the jester in a sarcastic tone, "You've never seen a jester kiss a princess before?" They all laughed, "Well not one so short." Wilber put his hand on the jester's shoulder, "You said we helped you to be brave when actually it tis the other way around, you have helped us not only be brave, but shown us that there are better people in this desolate world we live in." The jester smiled at him and with this they turned to walk back towards the castle. "Wait, there is something that I do not understand," Taylor said, shaking his head, "was Dufor and Dylan one in the same? Was he always a sorcerer or dragon?" Nicholas looked at him and with the kindness of words said, "He was always a sorcerer."

Taylor shook his head then turned to walk with the others. In the back of his mind he still could not comprehend what happened. He reflected to when the dragon first came. He remembered the dragon had shown up and for some unknown reason he had eaten the queen. Dufor had eaten the queen he thought to himself again. What had the king done after this act? He puzzled again; he had married Esmeralda that news had traveled far because of the nature of the courtship. He stopped dead in his tracks. "Wait" he said, "where is the queen, did the king get her to safety before the dragon attacked?" Nicholas turned to look at him, now a puzzled look on his face. "I never thought of that, I wonder if he did." Wilbur looked at him, "You are after all the king's bravest knight, he would have entrusted you with such a task, did he not?"

Nicholas shook his head no. "As a matter of fact, the queen sent me out to look for the sorcerer because before the dragon came, he had fled, which makes perfect sense now." Fornshell, who had been listening this whole time finally spoke up. "So, you are telling us that before the dragon attacked, the queen sent you to look for the sorcerer, leaving the king by himself to do battle? Is that what you are saying?" Nicholas thought for a moment, then shook his head yes in response. The jester, not sure why this subject had any meaning at all, looked at Taylor. "What are you getting at?"

Taylor looked at all of them, he did not know if he should say what was on his mind at all because it seemed so far-fetched. "The queen, it makes perfect sense to me, the queen did this, all of this." The princess shook her head, "That is not possible, she has been nothing but a good mother and a good wife this whole time." Taylor spoke again, "I do not believe that the sorcerer conjured up this thing by himself. Think about this. There was no trouble until the dragon showed up. He ate your mother. Then he took away our bodies and put a spell on us that bound us to the black forest all this time so that we would not be here. Then all of a sudden, the dragon is gone, and your father marries Esmerelda, a villager. Why?"

They all stood there for a moment. At first it didn't make any sense, then Taylor spoke again. "We all know that Dylan was not that good of a sorcerer, he never had power like this, he bungled everything. How could he have transformed himself into a dragon?" "I'll tell you." Came a voice from behind. They all spun and turned to see Esmeralda standing behind them. "I wondered how long it would be before anyone figured this out. It was I who helped Dylan. I gave him the power to become a dragon. I gave him the idea." "But why? "asked the princess, her voice in shock. Esmeralda laughed; her voice almost inhuman. "Because I wanted to rule this kingdom. And I have waited all this time." Her voice grew darker as she spoke. "I met with Dylan, I promised him you on your twentieth birthday if he would help me carry this out.
He fell in love with me though and I hated him for it just as I hated you and your father. Centuries I have waited for this moment, and what did you do? You of all people had to send that jester to the dark forest.

There was nothing I could do to prevent it." Was it just their imagination, or did she seem to be getting taller as she spoke? Wilber rubbed his eyes and thought he must be imagining it. "It was

I who cursed you to the dark forest. It was I who devoured your dear mother. It was I who made Dylan the dragon he is. And it is I that will send you to your doom." Thunder boomed and lightning struck Esmeralda.

"Oh shit!" Fornshell cried as he backed away, the others in tow. Esmeralda began to take on another form. They watched in horror as she began to change. Her hands began to change, turning from human hands to dark black long dangly fingers. Her face began to glow with a red color and her grin turned devilishly evil. Her eyes, once a vision of heavenly blue now changed to fire red. Her hair began to fall out of her skull and large bumps took its place. Her fair skin turning black with streaks of crimson. Her laugh boomed louder as her teeth formed into large fangs, her tongue now almost snake-like. The jester backed away and bumped into Taylor, "What is she?" the jester asked. Taylor, looking dumbfounded shrugged his shoulders. Esmeralda, now three times her normal size, looked like a hideous demon, she reached out and grabbed Wilber by the neck and raised him off the ground to meet her fiery eyes. "Do you like me this way?" she asked. Wilber, unable to speak as her grip was choking him, shook his head no. She laughed again, "I wait no longer, I take what is rightfully mine." And with that she dropped Wilber to the ground. He scrambled backwards, clutching his throat and trying to regain his breath.

The jester walked towards her, "Who are you?" he asked. She looked down at him, and with an evil smile she spoke, "I am Hellmervick, the black demon, the one who was trapped centuries ago. I sat in that awful chamber for decades planning and waiting to take over this kingdom, this forest, and now I will have my revenge." The jester stood there, scared out of wits. "How did you escape? The legend is that you were buried there in the roots of the great tree, how could you have been released?" The demon smiled. The jester felt a sharp object pierce his back, he stiffened losing his grip on his sword. He fell to his knees and looked behind him. Nicholas stood there. He pushed the jester out of his way, and he knelt on one knee. "I have served you well master, what is your reward for me?" Hellmervick looked down at him and in a great voice said to him, "You shall rule by my side"

ELEVEN

The jester slowly opened his eyes, at first everything seemed dark and gloomy. Something felt wet behind him, but he could not reach out to touch it, his hands were bound. The smell of smoke hung heavy in the air and he could barely make out what looked like torches on the wall near him. He heard a gasp to his right and he turned his head to see who it was. Shackled to the wall next to him was the princess. His eyes adjusted to the light and he could see that he was in the king's dungeon. He could make out the figures of Wilber, Fornshell, and Taylor who were also shackled to the wall across from him. "We thought you were dead." The princess said in a weak and fearful voice. "I believe he only wounded me." He said, his voice groggy and frail. "How are we to get out of here?" Wilber looked at him, his eyes full of despair, "I do not know, this chamber was built to be escape proof, there are two guards posted outside, and we are bound and unable to loosen ourselves." The jester thought for a moment, "Why did Nicholas let the demon out? What could have been his motive, wasn't he the kings best knight?" Taylor looked at him, the jester could almost see his brain working through his eyes. "We worked together, we fought together, he did not seem jealous, he seemed to really love the king, as a matter of fact he made a promise to never let the king down. I don't understand why he would do this, why he would help that fowl creature to take over this kingdom. It doesn't make any sense to me."

"I have been thinking about this a lot," added Fornshell, "I have concluded that he must have been tempted somehow. We all know the story about the demon and his thirst to rule this kingdom. The painting on the wall in the great hall also foretold that he would be released, and the jester would save us. I don't understand why he would release him. And why wait 20 years when he could have easily destroyed all of us. What could this all mean?" They all stared in silence, none of them speaking. Then Wilber spoke, his voice in urgency, "I know" he said, "I remember an elder of the black forest who told me the story of Hellmervick before he died. There was a wizard, his name was Kali. He created an obsidian chamber that would hold the demon. In order to get him inside of it he had to trick him. There was a great battle, he kept up the pretense in order to convince him he was not lying. In the battle Kali gave up his life. But there is something else. Kali had a daughter and she vowed vengeance for the death of her father. She was the only one who knew where the chamber was hidden."

"What are you saying?" the jester asked impatiently. "This," Wilber continued, "I believe that Nicholas is an heir of Kali, how else would he be able to free the demon. How else would he know where the chamber was hidden?" "So you believe that he dug up the chamber, released the demon, who then came up with a master plan, met with Dylan, promised him the princess, ate the queen, married the king, and now has brought nothing but doom and disparity to the kingdom? Why would I do that?" "The answer is complicated, yet I do not know." Wilber said with a shrug of his shoulders. "But I believe I can get us out of here." "How?" cried the princess, "My great great grandfather made this place unbreakable." "My right hand is free, I do not know how, but I am not bound." He quickly began working feverishly on his left hand. After about ten minutes he broke the lock free, and the shackles fell to the ground. He stood up quickly, watching the gate for the guards as he freed the other warriors. "How was your hand free?" the jester asked. "I don't know, it was like the shackle fell off, like it was loose on purpose. But that does not matter now, we must hurry, we must destroy the demon."

"Wait," said the jester, "we can't just go waltzing out there, we have no plan, you cannot destroy a demon, and even if we did, we have no tools for it." Wilber looked at the jester with a strange smile. He began working feverishly to free the others from their shackles. "Don't you know? You are the one in the painting, you are the one who will defeat the demon, and you are the one that was prophesied about centuries ago. That is why you were sent to the black forest, that is why you came to Lavodka, and that is why the demon is afraid of you." "He didn't look afraid of me before, what makes you think all this, I thought that painting was about the dragon? There is something you are not telling me, what the hell is it?" Wilber went over to the gate, he cautiously peered out looking for the guards. He saw that all was clear and that the guards were at the entrance to the dungeon by the other gate. He looked around the floor for something he could use as a weapon, and then he saw it, a large wooden object. He motioned for Fornshell to grab a torch off the wall as he picked up the wooden beam. It felt heavy in his hands and he believed he could use this to render the guards unconscious.

He went back to the gate and saw that it was locked, but the lock looked rusty. He knew that if he hit the lock it would bring the guards rushing towards them, so he grabbed it. It gave way under the pressure of his grip and fell to the floor. He saw a guard turn to look his way and he ducked back into the cell. When he felt it was clear again, he quietly opened the gate. He motioned for the others to follow him and quietly they walked towards the guards. He steadied the beam in his hands and as he approached the guards, he hit one on the back of the head. As the guard fell to the ground the other guard swiftly turned to face Wilber. But Fornshell was on him in a matter of seconds pushing the torch into his face. He backed away from the fire and Wilbur hit him over the head. With a mighty thunk, the guard was on the floor. Wilber paused to see if anyone else was going to approach, but the hallway beyond was silent. "Okay" he whispered, "This is way too easy, either they have set a trap for us, or...." He paused not finishing his statement. He turned towards the gate and it was not locked. He pushed it open and walked out into the dimly lit hallway. He could see the stone steps that led from the cavern to the first floor of the castle. With his beam set to the ready, he motioned for the others to follow. The princess clutched onto the jester as if her life depended on it. Taylor stayed in the back watching the rear in case anyone was behind them hiding in the shadows.

They started to climb the winding staircase when they heard the great steel door at the top of the steps open. They stopped, Wilber ready for battle, the others close by. They heard the door shut again and could hear heavy footfalls as someone descended the steps. Wilber motioned for them to go back down, and they all began to walk backwards, watching ahead of them in great anticipation. Suddenly they were face to face with Nicholas, Wilber raised the beam to strike him when Nicholas cried out. "Don't." he said, with an urgency in his voice. Wilber stopped. "It is not as you think," Nicholas said, "I am on your side, I have been from the start." "Then it's true," said the jester, "You are a descendant of Kali." "Yes, I have been planning my revenge on Hellmervick since I was a small child. Our family has been wanting to destroy him for ages, but we had to wait till this time, we had to wait until now." With that he tossed the sword to the jester. "It was foretold eons ago that the jester with the red hair would be the one who could destroy the demon. But the demon did not know this as he was imprisoned in the chamber that Kali had assembled. Only the enchanted ones and my family knew. Only when the princess sent the jester did Esmeralda fully understand, as there was some knowledge he had, but was unable to stop it. Once the demon was outside of the magical barrier of the black forest, he could no longer enter."

"I am supposed to kill him with this?" He held up the sword. "I thought this was only for the dragon?" He asked in bewilderment. "It holds great power." Wilber added, "It will send him back to whence he came." The jester looked at the sword then looked at

Wilber again. "And how am I supposed to get close enough to even use it?" "There is a way." Said Nick, "There is a secret tunnel that leads to the Kings chambers, I will show you." With that he turned and started up the stone staircase. "Wait," said the jester, "how will this sword send him back?" Nick turned to the jester and after a long pause spoke to him. "Kali had forged this sword and cast a great spell on it.

When the words are spoken the sword will glow with a burning golden color. But I must tell you, he is no ordinary demon, he has the power to be anything he wants, anything! To send him back where he came from you must sever his head, it is the only way otherwise he will only appear dead, he can be reborn as anything he wishes, anytime, anywhere, anyplace. But you must cut off his head to send him back where he came from." "And where is that?" The jester asked. Nick thought for a moment, then he turned back towards the exit. "The time is short, and I do not have time to explain."

TWELVE

Hellmervick, back in the form of Esmeralda, sat in the king's chamber. She was softly humming to herself when there came a knock on the door. "Enter." The door opened and the Bishop walked in. He looked at her as she combed her hair while looking into a rather large mirror. "What do you want Bishop? Speak and make it fast." The Bishop stepped a little closer, "My Queen, with the dragon destroyed and the conspirators captured, when shall we have the execution?" She smiled as she looked at herself in the mirror, "This afternoon." The Bishop cleared his throat and in a shy voice asked, "And what of the Kings daughter?" She turned sharply and faced the Bishop, her eyes almost burning red, "If she had not gone to the Jester and those men from the Black Forest her father would not be dead now, now would he?"

She almost seemed to growl at the Bishop. He lowered his head, "No, I believe not." "Then she must too die, they all must be beheaded, you will call for the executioner and they will be taken care of this afternoon, now, do you have any other business?" The Bishop shook his head no, and with that he left the room. Hellmervick sat back a smile crawling across the face of the beautiful Esmeralda. The plan that was formed so long ago was starting to come together. Sitting in the obsidian chamber for what seemed like eons had given him enough time to come up with a full proof plan. How delighted he was to be set free, how incredibly delighted indeed. Now that the king was dead, he could be ruler over the whole country. Soon the only other people in his way would be dead as well, how wonderfully enthralling that will be.

The jester plugged his nose as he followed Nick through the damp dark passageway. He could not imagine what could be causing the foul order that hung heavy in the air. The stench was so bad it reminded him of a dead animal he once found on one of his journeys. He was returning from Briorwood, a castle in the far north where he had been performing, when he accidently made a wrong turn and ended up in a desolate place known as The Thickens. It was a dense forest populated with strange wild animals. Trying desperately to find his way out, he stumbled across a creature that had to have been dead for some time. He had never smelled anything so disgusting in his whole life, until now. Suddenly Nick stopped and the jester bumped into him. "The entrance is just ahead; this passage was built for the King to escape if there ever was a revolt. As you can see, it has never had to be used until now." The jester nodded his head, still trying to understand how he could be the chosen one. He thought for a moment. The painting on the wall of the cave in the black forest, how could that have been him? Why was he the chosen one? He didn't have any special skills. All he ever did was tell jokes and make people laugh. Was he supposed to tickle this demon to death?

Nick started walking again until he came to what looked like a stone door carved into the side of the passageway. "This is it." He said as he held the torch near the door. "There is a small hole here. You reach inside and there will be a small knob. Once you feel the knob, turn it slowly to the left. If you turn it too fast, the door will open quickly, spoiling your surprise." The jester shook his head. Nick turned to leave. "Wait," the jester blurted out, "where the hell do you think you are going?" Nick looked at him and with the calmest of voices said, "You have to do this alone, only you can do this; it is your destiny."

The jester widened his eyes, "You have got to be kidding? Why am I the chosen one? Why can't it be someone else's destiny, like Fornshell or Wilber? Why am I the only one who can do this?" Nick put his hand on the jester's shoulder and spoke as quietly as he could. "You my friend know something that no one else knows. It was foretold by the prophets and magical people of the Black Forest. I cannot tell you anything else other than this is your destiny and you must do it alone. Now you must hurry, we haven't much time." Nick turned and left. The jester stood there, his mouth hanging open. What the hell was he talking about? What did he know that nobody else knew?

He stood there puzzling. He looked down at the sword, then at the hole where the knob was. "Well, I guess I might as well get this over with, I ain't getting any younger." And with that he stuck his hand in the hole. He felt around until he found the knob. Once his hand was on it, he grabbed it firmly, closed his eyes, and then began to turn it slowly to the left. Dust began to fall from the stone door as it slowly creaked open. When it was open just enough to let him through, he stopped turning the knob. He peered through the door and he could see the kings' chambers. He saw a large bed made with silk linens and colorful drapes that hung around the sides. He slowly stepped in and he could see the room lay empty. The demon, or Esmeralda, or Hellmervick, or whatever it called itself, was not in the room.

The jester saw that to the right of the bed chambers led to another room, he thought that it must be the changing room. Across the room to the left was another door, this one was closed. He thought that it must lead to the Kings sitting room and the hallway to the castle. As quietly as he could he headed for the changing room first. If it was empty, he would go to the other door.

Trying to not to make any noise at all, he approached the changing room. The door was already open, so he peered inside. Again, it was empty. His first thought was that Nick really wasn't on his side and they had laid a trap for him. He tried to shake off this feeling and then his mind went back to what Nick had said. "You know something no one else knows." What could he possibly know that nobody else knew? He squinted his eyes trying to think his whole life over. He was the son of a jester, his father was the son of a jester, but his great grandfather was a knight. He didn't know how to be funny. The jester thought to himself, his grandfather used to tell him stories of his great grandfather. He was a knight in a faraway kingdom and fought great battles with dragons and sorcerers and he didn't know how to be funny. What was that story he told? He kept thinking to himself, racking his brain, but he couldn't remember the story.

Suddenly he was taken back to a warm summer day when he was a child. His red hair dark and his skin as smooth as silk. He lay in the grass looking up at the sky when his grandfather walked to him. "Hello my boy." His grandfather said to him smiling, his long white beard flapping in the breeze. The boy looked up at him and smiled, his grin from ear to ear, "Hello grandfather, do you have a story for me today?" His grandfather smiled like he never smiled before, his grin as delightful as the morning sun when it glistened on the dew. "But of course, my boy, come sit on my lap and I will tell you the story of the bravest knight in all the land." The boy smiled because he knew that grandfather loved to tell this story, it was his favorite story to tell. He jumped up and walked with his grandfather to a tree stump. His grandfather sat down and adjusted his garments, then the boy sat on his lap and looked up eagerly at his grandfather.

"It happened long ago in a country far away, a country you may go to someday my boy, but don't let me get ahead of myself. There was a great demon that tried to rule over this vast kingdom of this faraway land and the only person who was brave enough to stop him was a great knight, a warrior, a knight with special powers because he was also a wizard. He was my Great, great grandfather father, your great, great, great grandfather, err, four greats, or something to that effect. He was the only one who battled with the demon and the only one smart enough to trick him. He built a chamber that would hold him for all of eternity. On the day of the great battle your great grandfather, my father, fought with him, he told him that the whole kingdom would be his if he could take the key from the chamber he had built. Of course, the fierce demon did not believe him, so he had to go into the chamber himself to show that he was not lying. When the demon went into the chamber after him your great grandfather struck him with a mighty blow from a sword that gave him great power, but it was not enough, and the demon fought back." The boy looked up at his grandfather with excitement in his eyes, "What did he do then grandfather?" the boy asked enthusiastically.

The grandfather looked down at his grandson, tears starting to fill up in his eyes. "He did what any noble knight would do my boy; he gave his own life to make sure that the demon would never escape." The boy suddenly looked sad, he raised his eyes again, "How?" The old man wiped away the tears from his eyes and drew in a deep breath. "Well my boy, as brave as he was, he closed the chamber door from the inside, locking himself and the demon in the chamber for all eternity." "But what if they escape, what if they both get out, wouldn't great grandfather still be alive?" the boy asked with a kind of excitement in his voice. The old man sat there for a moment and thought long and hard, then he suddenly burst into laughter. "No my boy, the one thing that the most noble of knights never had was a sense of humor and what he didn't know was the demon, if he laughed, if he even cracked a smile, it would bring down his guard to the point that he could be beheaded, and that my boy, is the only way to truly kill this demon."

Suddenly the door from the sitting room flew open and Esmeralda stood at the door, her eyes like two wildfires burning out of control. She looked at the jester as if she wanted to eat him for lunch. "How did you escape?" She screamed at the top of her lungs. The jester stood there, frozen, he could not speak or move. "No matter, I will just kill you myself." She raised her hand and lightning expelled from the tips of her fingers. The jester moved like he never moved before and raised his sword. The lightning reflected off the sword and struck the chamber wall instead. Esmeralda looked in disbelief and raised her hand to do it again. But the jester, who was much smaller than she, and as quick as lightning himself, moved to the other side of the room. "I know your secret." the Jester said as he moved back and forth, watching Esmeralda's every move. "Secret? Ha, I have none, I only have hate for you!" "Like the hate you had for my great, great, great, great, great grandfather?" The jester hissed. Esmeralda stopped dead in her tracks. She looked at the Jester with a look of bewilderment and disgust all at once. She sneered at the Jester, her face contorting like a dying animal. "Your what?" she said with a disgusted voice. The Jester grinned, his eyes suddenly gleaming, "Kali, you know, that old man that disguised himself as a knight." Esmeralda looked at the jester, her eyes now like two slits on her contorted face. "Kali, the powerful wizard, the great knight, related........to you?" she cried out. Suddenly she broke into uncontrollable laughter. The jester could not believe it, she was laughing. He took no time to take this all in and thrust towards her, his sword in the ready. He leapt at her and with one swing he hit her throat from the left, swinging it through until the sword completed its task and in one swift motion, Esmeralda's head detached from her body and fell to the floor with a loud thunk.

The jester took a step back, as the body of Esmeralda began to sink to the floor. He looked at her head laying on the floor. Her face in utter shock, her mouth trying to move as if to speak, but nothing came out. The light in her eyes slowly fading to nothing. Smoke began to flow from the severed neck and the body began to look as if it was deflating. The jester watched as the life of Hellmervick slowly left and the body moved no more. He breathed a heavy sigh of relief and dropped the sword to the floor. He heard a rustling outside the door and decided to see what was going on. He walked to the other side of the chamber to the door that led to the hall. He could hear fighting as he approached the door. He crept it open slowly and peered into the hallway. He could see Wilber, Fornshell, Taylor and Nick fighting with Queens guards. He went back, picked up the sword and went into the hallway to join in the battle.

Taylor looked and saw him, "What kept you?" The jester, about to hit one of the guards, looked at him, "Oh you know, the usual, beheading demons and such." Taylor smiled as he slid his sword into the breast of the guards. As the last guard hit the floor they all looked at each other, and with a great smile they all laughed. "So, the demon is dead?" Wilber asked. The jester looked at him and with a great sigh shook his head yes. "Well then, let us bury the body, the head separate from the body, just in case."

The jester looked at him, "In case, just in case, just in case of what?" he asked. Wilber smiled at him, "you just never know."

They all walked into the kings chambers and saw the headless body of Hellmervick on the floor. "Well," said Taylor, "he surely looks dead.' He took his sword and moved the head with it. Nothing happened and Taylor stepped back. "We should buy this in the south garden, and the head we should destroy." Said Nick. The jester looked at Nick in great amusement, "We are related, did you know?" Nick looked at the jester and with a large smile he nodded. The jester suddenly frowned, "Why didn't you tell me? That was a pretty rotten trick!" Nick smiled, "As I said, there was no time." He patted the jester on his back and gave out a hardy laugh. The jester smiled as he looked up, he saw the figure of the princess walk into the room. His smile faded as he looked at her and silence fell on the room as everyone began to stare. She looked at the jester and she lowered her head. Wilber looked at his comrades and with a short turn of his head towards the door they all left.

The princess walked over to the jester and put her hand on his cheek and gently tilted his head to meet her gaze. "And do you still feel the same of me?" she asked. The jester looked at her for a moment. The love he had in his heart for her burst from his chest like a frog leaping into a pond, and he could feel his heartbeat jump into his throat. "I do, if thou will still have me, after all I am only a jester." She looked at him and smiled, "I have always loved you my jester." A frown came on her face, "Jester, I only know you as jester. What is thy name?" The jester looked at her and with a smile on his face and a twinkle in his eye he said, 'My name oh lady, is Aaron." They embraced in a kiss. The jester thought to himself, this was what he wanted more than anything in the world.

EPILOGUE

A new era had fallen over the land. The jester and the princess were married and together they rebuilt the castle, and the kingdom was the happiest it had been in many years. Wilber, Taylor, and Fornshell were re-knighted and took their place next to the new king, king Aaron. Nick became the commander over all the knights and the land had peace like it had never seen before.

The enchanted creatures of the Black Forest returned and harmony between those and the people of the land was the best it had ever been. All seemed well in the land. Wilber stood on the balcony of the knight's chamber looking over the land, his mind wandering to the most recent events. Everything was great, yet something did not feel right. He pondered this for a moment, something felt wrong. He could not put his finger on it. It had been more than a year since they slain Hellmervick and there was peace. Still, something simmered in the back of his head that he just could not let go. He turned and walked into the castle.

"What is amiss?" asked Taylor, who was sitting in the far-left corner of the chamber, sharpening his sword. 'Something does not feel right, like something we missed." "I don't know what you would be talking about. The dragon is dead, Hellmervick is dead, and we buried his head in a different spot than his body. What could possibly be wrong?" Wilber thought for a moment but did not say anything. He gave Taylor a quick glance then walked out of the room and headed for the Kings chambers.

He knocked once and heard the king bid him enter. He walked into the chamber and saw the king sitting at a table, his bright red hair glowing like fire. "What can I do for you Wilber?" he said happily. Wilber thought for a moment, then proceeded carefully. "I beg your pardon sire, but can you tell me what happened when you slain the demon?" Aaron looked at him and with a smile said, "Well, when I told him that I was related to Kali, he just broke down and started laughing. I had remembered a story that my grandfather used to tell me, that the only way to kill this demon was to get it to laugh, it would let its guard down and was able to be killed. At that moment I cut off his head."

Wilber stood there for a moment still pondering, then his face lit up like he had remembered something he had forgotten to ask before. "The words, you said the magical words before you swung, yes?" Aaron thought for a moment, a look of confusion on his face, 'Yes, I believe so." Wilber lunged forward and grabbed Aaron, "You believe so, or you know so?" He asked in an angry tone. Aaron shuddered, he shook his head, "I..I..am not sure, but it was dead." Wilber let go of the king. "No no no no no," he shouted, "if you had said the words the sword would have sealed the body and the soul could not have escaped. Did smoke escape from out of the body?"

Aaron thought back, he remembered seeing the smoke come from the severed neck. He hung his head low, "Yes." Wilber turned to face the king. "Not to worry, if he wanted us he would be here again." Wilber lowered his head, "It is okay, rookie mistake, but we must never let our guard down. He can come back anytime, any-place, as anything he wants, anything." Aaron stood there pondering this thought as Wilber left the room, his words echoing down the hall, the word anything, like an axe chopping at a tree. Any-thing. Anything. Anything. Anything.

The End?

PRESENT DAY

Professor Brock raised his head and looked at the jet he was about to board. He thought back to his days as an archeologist, he always enjoyed finding ancient artifacts, but since he had been older, he had restrained from going on such adventures. It had been almost twenty years since the last time he went to an actual site. It was in Egypt, he had been part of a small team that had discovered the tomb of Inclarie, a Pharaoh who had died at an early age. Inclarie was thought of as only a legend, so finding his tomb was a monumental occasion.

He smiled to himself as he thought about where he was going this time. Another legend, the fabled black knight of Spain, and evil knight that lived in a castle just north of what is now the city of Madrid, was fabled to be a demon who drank the blood of his victims. He shuddered at the thought, an ancient evil vampire. When the remains of an ancient castle were uncovered less than a week ago during a freak storm, he was eager to take on the role of lead archeologist. No one had found the entrance to the castle yet, so Brock was excited to get there. He could feel his body tremble as he began to board the jet. His thoughts racing about what he would find. Would he find the legend was true, would he find a tomb? He thought back to the legend. The year was 1540, the story goes that there was a knight who came from nowhere. He took over an abandoned castle and began to make war with anyone who opposed him. His goal was to rule over the land, so it was told. He would raid the local villages and kill his victims by draining and drinking their blood. Again, Brock shuddered at how gruesome this was. Finally, the villagers had enough and tracked down the black knight. According to legend, they tracked him down to his castle, overpowered him somehow, and cut off his head. Story is that they buried his body in the castle and placed his head in a secret location away from the castle.

When they were done a great storm raged through the land and the castle was destroyed, then what remained was covered by the earth, never to be seen again. Such a wild story, no evidence was found to substantiate this legend, until recently.

ACKNOWLEDGEMENT

I would like to acknowledge my children, Aaron, Nicholas, and Taylor for allowing me to use their names in this work of fiction.
My children have always been a huge inspiration for me to do the things that I have always wanted to and to never give up. I also want to acknowledge Tammy Cornelius, my wife for the last 27 years who encouraged me to go to college, inspired me to never give up, and to always go for the things that I have always dreamed about.
I also would like to acknowledge my manager at my former job who would encourage me to write little snippets when I would send out an email every day to those I worked with. It was while writing these daily emails where I came up with the story for The Black Forest, as it was a small two-week serial that related to our lunch menu. Also, others who worked at the with me there were inspirations for characters that were also in this book.

Namely the characters of Fornshell and Wilber, you know who are. Also, the fact that you all wanted to read this story I was writing in small snippets every day, without this I could not have fleshed out this small book.
I want to acknowledge my sister who passed in 2007. She would have loved to see this accomplishment and I miss her very much. And if there is anyone, I forgot in the dedication page of my book or on this acknowledgement page, it is not that you are forgotten,

it is just I can not name everyone.

I also want to thank those who have already read my book, without you I would not be able to continue to do this, so from the bottom of my heart, thank you so much.

ABOUT THE AUTHOR

Miles Cornelius

James Walter Miles Cornelius is originally from Porterville California where he grew up. He attended Alta Vista Elementery school where he gratuated in 1982. He attendted Porterville High School from 1982-1986. In 1988 he moved to Oregon and joined the Navy in 1990 and was a cook for four years. In 2001 he went to college at Eastern Oregon University where he earned a Bachelors Degree of Science in Liberal Studies with minors in Anthropology\Sociology and Health.

PRAISE FOR AUTHOR

Once I started reading this book I could not put it down. I am waiting for his next book to come out.

- TY MARLOW

2

Made in the USA
Middletown, DE
30 September 2021